Anonymous

Report of the Proceedings of the Meeting of the Bishop, Clergy and Laity of the Diocese of Quebec

SALZWASSER VERLAG

Anonymous

Report of the Proceedings of the Meeting of the Bishop, Clergy and Laity of the Diocese of Quebec

Reprint of the original, first published in 1859.

1st Edition 2022 | ISBN: 978-3-37513-186-9

Verlag (Publisher): Salzwasser Verlag GmbH, Zeilweg 44, 60439 Frankfurt, Deutschland
Vertretungsberechtigt (Authorized to represent): E. Roepke, Zeilweg 44, 60439 Frankfurt, Deutschland
Druck (Print): Books on Demand GmbH, In de Tarpen 42, 22848 Norderstedt, Deutschland

REPORT

OF THE

PROCEEDINGS OF THE MEETING

OF THE

Bishop, Clergy and Laity

OF THE

DIOCESE OF QUEBEC,

HELD AT THE

NATIONAL SCHOOL HOUSE, QUEBEC,

ON THE 24th JUNE, 1858.

TAKEN FROM THE "QUEBEC MERCURY" OF THE 26th OF THAT MONTH ;

TOGETHER WITH CERTAIN ARTICLES FROM THAT JOURNAL, AND OTHERS, BEARING UPON THE SUBJECT OF

SYNODICAL ACTION.

QUEBEC :
PRINTED AT THE MERCURY OFFICE.

1859.

*** No pains having been spared to give circulation
 newspapers and pamphlets setting forth a particular
lass of views on subjects connected with Synodical
ction, it has been thought desirable to collect to-
ether, and republish, certain articles which have
ppeared from time to time, in the Quebec Mercury,
id Chronicle, and other papers, on the opposite
de of the question. It will be important to observe
at the two journals just mentioned are the only
cular papers in Quebec which, through their Edi-
rs or Proprietors, are connected with the Church
 England, although neither of them is under the
fluence, in the least degree, of any ecclesiastical
thority ; and they therefore may be reasonably sup-
sed to represent the opinions of the majority of the
embers of that Church.

In the articles which follow, some slight omissions
ve been made of passages which are either inap-
opriate in the present state of things, or too per-
nal in their character to make it desirable to
publish them.

REPORT, &c.

From the Quebec Mercury, 26th of June, 1858.

SYNOD MEETING OF THE CLERGY AND LAITY OF THE CHURCH OF ENGLAND.

The general meeting of members of the Anglican Church, of which a brief report was given up to the hour of our last publication, was attended by the greater portion, though not all, of the Clergy of the Diocese, and about one hundred and fifty lay members, of whom not more than ten had come in from the country parishes specially for the meeting.

His Lordship the Bishop, as a [...]ter of course occupied the chair, and the Rev. S. Wood ope: the meeting by reading several appropriate prayers.

The Lord Bishop in introducing the subject which had called the meeting together, said, that by permission of Almighty God they had met for the purpose of considering and adopting the act of parliament by which synodical powers had been conferred on the bishop, clergy and laity of the church of England, and framing a constitution and regulations for the government of the church. His Lordship remarked that for a period of sixty-five years the affairs of the church had been conducted without the exercise of this power, and it was but very lately that the subject of synodical action had been prominently brought forward. In 1851 the initiatory movement was made in the matter by five bishops who assembled in Quebec; he mentioned the fact of the subject having originated amongst the Bishops, as an evidence of the confidence placed by them in the laity. The adoption of certain regulations and resolutions was the first step taken. Two years afterwards his Lordship went to England for the purpose of meeting the metropolitan of Australia (the Lord Bishop of Sydney,) to consult the highest authorities at home and to obtain power to act in the matter from the Imperial Parliament. Objections, however, arose in England as to the eligibility of that course of procedure, and it was afterward thought proper to apply to the Provincial Legislature. The act, to adopt which they had met, was the consequence of that application ; it had received the sanction of royalty, and the power of Synodical action had thus been constituted. His Lordship said that the present meeting was not a synod, but simply a meeting to prepare the way for the formation of a synod ; and in the furtherance of this object, he had availed himself of the assistance of several gentlemen to draw up certain resolutions, which would be submitted to the consideration of the meeting. The first resolution had merely reference to the adoption by this meeting of the Act of Parliament ; the second was for the purpose of establishing the principle of representation in the synod when formed, and it was open to all persons, members of the church, to propose such alterations therein, and amendments thereto, as were consistent with the general principles which governed the church. He hoped and trusted that the consideration of the subject and the action taken upon it by this meeting would be such as would receive the approbation of the church, the clergy, and the laity of the Church of England, not only through all the places whose interests are identified in that action, but throughout the world ; and that whatever discussion took place it would be marked by that cool and calm reflection, that christian candour and gentleness, corresponding with the importance of the subject, and not with minds clouded or prejudiced by personal ideas or considerations. His Lordship concluded by saying that they would now proceed to consider what that synodical action would be, without which they had done for sixty-five years ; and he hoped that the first steps taken would be successful ones. Referring again to the fact that the movement originated with the bishops, and the feeling towards the laity manifested by their so doing, he sat down.

Revd. A. W. Mountain, was appointed Secretary to the meeting, and read the following Act of the Provincial Parliament authorizing Synodical Action :—

Act to enable the Members of the United Church of England and Ireland in Canada, to meet in Synod. (19 & 20 Vic., cap. 141, Passed by both houses of Imperial Parliament, 13th June, 1856.)

Whereas, doubts exist whether the members of the United Church of England and Ireland, in this Province, have the power of regulating the affairs of their Church in matters relating to discipline, and necessary to order and good government, and it is just that such doubts should be removed in order that they may be permitted to exercise the same rights of self government that are enjoyed by other religious communities ; therefore, Her Majesty, by and with the advice and consent of the Legislative Council and Assembly of Canada, enacts as follows :—

1. The Bishops, Clergy, and Laity, members of the United Church of England and Ireland, in this Province, may meet in their several Dioceses, which are now, or may be hereafter constituted in this Province, and in such manner and by such proceedings as they shall adopt, frame constitutions, and make regulations for enforcing discipline in the Church, for the appointment, deposition, deprivation, or removal of any person bearing office therein, of whatever order or degree, any rights of the Crown to the contrary notwithstanding, for the convenient and orderly management of the property, affairs and interests of the Church in matters relating to and affecting only the said Church, and the officers and members thereof, and not in any manner interfering with the rights, privileges or interests of other religious communities, or of any person or persons not being a member or members of the said United Church of England and Ireland ; Provided always that such constitutions and regulations shall apply only to the Diocese or Dioceses adopting the same.

II The Bishops, Clergy, and Laity, members of the United Church of England and Ireland, in this Province, may meet in general Assembly within this Province, by such Representatives as shall be determined and declared by them in their several Dioceses ; and in such general Assembly frame a constitution and regulations for the general management and good government of the said Church in this Province ; provided always, that nothing in this act contained shall authorise the imposition of any rate or tax upon any person or persons whomsoever, whether belonging to the said Church or not, or the infliction of any punishment, fine, or penalty upon any person, other than his suspension or removal from an office in the said Church or exclusion from the meetings or proceedings of the Diocesan or General Synods ; and provided also, nothing in the said constitution, regulations, or any of them, shall be contrary to any law or statutes now or hereafter in force in this Province.

It was then moved by the Hon. W. Sheppard, seconded by the Revd. D. Falloon, D. D.

1.—That we, the Bishop, Clergy, and Laity of the Doicese of Quebec legally convened, adopt the Act of the Provincial Parliament entitled " An Act to enable the members of the United Church of England and Ireland to meet in Synod."

The first resolution was then put to the meeting and unanimously adopted.

The second Resolution was proposed by the Revd. S. S. Wood, M.A., seconded by the Revd. E. C. Parkin.

2.—That pending the adoption of a constitution by the Synod at its first meeting, the Synod shall consist of the Bishop of the Diocese, of the clergy of the same, being in Priests Orders, instituted or licensed to the cure of souls, or being Principals or Professors of Divinity in any College, or being head masters of Schools under the jurisdiction (in either case) of the Bishop, and not being under ecclesiastical censure : and of lay Representatives, as hereafter to be provided.

Revd. Mr. Wood said, in moving the resolution, that he hoped it would not meet with opposition, as he disliked opposition very much. There were occasions when an open and manly opposition was required, and no one admired more than he did opposition of that nature ; the opposition he disliked was that of a factious nature, and he hoped that nothing of that description would characterize the proceedings of the present meeting. He was not much in favor of long speeches, and indeed there was nothing in the resolution which would enable a person to make a long speech upon it.

Mr. Jeffrey Hale here rose and said that he had an amendment to propose. The idea of this amendment had arisen in his mind from what he had heard at that meeting, and of course, he had not yet put it upon paper. Previous to doing so, he would explain the opinion which, although he was no lawyer, he entertained on the subject under discussion. He doubted very much whether this meeting could delegate its power of forming a constitution to any other parties. The act distinctly stated that the bishop, clergy, and laity of the Church of England must meet and frame their constitution and regulations themselves ; no one else could frame the constitution. In laying the foundation of our edifice therefore it would be but wise to lay it surely. The body mentioned in the resolution just read, might, it is true, frame a constitution and regulations ; but that constitution and those regulations would not be the constitution or regulations of the Church of England in synod assembled, and might, consequently, be easily affected, and difficulties would arise which would be very hard to get over. This meeting was called together for the purpose of framing a constitution and regulations for the government of the Church, for the delegation of their power to do so to another body the act made no provision whatever. He would therefore respectfully suggest that those gentlemen even although they possessed much more wisdom than he did, had, in framing the resolution, followed a course not in accordance with the provisions of the Act of Parliament. He would therefore, move an amendment to the following effect :—

That a committee consisting of twelve members, be appointed by ballot for the purpose of framing the draft of a constitution for the regulation of the Church of England of this diocese ; the same to be submitted to a public meeting of the members of the Church of England of this diocese for their sanction and approval, at such date as might be decided on.

Mr. George Hall, the acting Mayor, begged permission to enquire whether Mr. Hale's opinion was supported by that of any of the legal gentlemen he saw present?

Mr. Andrew Stuart, advocate, having then been called upon by the unanimous voice of the meeting to give his opinion on the subject, said :—That the Act gave the church powers of government as described in the second clause of that document, by means of the bishop, clergy, and laity, and therefore, that a constitution for its government must be given by the members of the church as therein designated. These members could, however, he thought, appoint a Committee to draft or draw up a constitution, the members of the church having full power to alter, accept, or reject such constitution, according as they thought proper. The Act conferred no powers of government on a Synod ; the church was to be governed alone by means of a constitution and regulations drawn up by the members designated as the bishop, clergy, and laity. He therefore concurred in the view of the Act taken by Mr. Hale.

The Revd Mr. Wood here begged permission to enquire of the Chair whether it was understood that the voting was to be by orders. This enquiry created a decided manifestation of opposition among the lay members present, from which moment the discussion became irregular, and our reporter was unable to note the proceedings with any thing like accuracy.

The question was repeatedly raised whether the meeting did not already constitute a Synod.

Mr. James Bell Forsyth maintained that such was the case from the moment that the first Resolution had been passed, and that, this point established, the right of the Clergy to vote by orders, could not be denied them.

The Revd. Mr. Parkin could not conceal his surprise that, constituted as the assemblage was in the proportion of twenty laity to one clergyman,—a feeling should exist against the right of the clergy to vote as they considered they had the right of doing.

Mr. Hall expressed his surprise that the clergy should wish to set themselves in a position adverse to the will of the laity.

Mr. Parkin maintained in reply, that the present meeting, constituted as it was, could not by any means be looked upon as a representation of the laity. He insisted that it was self-evident, the clergy were members of the Church of England, while proof was requisite that every layman was a member of that church.

The Bishop stated that it was his conviction that, the clergy having with one voice decided against the motion of Mr. Hale, the amendment was rejected.

The cry of " question," on Mr. Hale's motion, being raised by Colonel Fitzgerald and other gentlemen,

The Bishop again stated that he was under the impression that the Clergy had declared their view on the subject.

The Lord Bishop here remarked that the words of the act were, with regard to Mr. Stuart's observation on the powers of Synods, that the bishop, clergy and laity " were to meet in Synod."

From this point in the discussion of the subject, an animated and by no means orderly system of debate prevailed, several clerical gentlemen opposing Mr. Hale's amendment, and maintaining that in no way could the government of the church be more efficiently worked out than by the formation of a Synod by the present meeting, and the further election and sending in of representatives from the different parishes, who would no doubt submit to the wishes of a constituted majority.

They opposed Mr. Hale's amendment on the principle that at present it would disfranchise the people of their parishes.

To this it was replied by Mr. Hale that no such intentions were entertained or shewn by the amendment ; it delegated no power to the committee which would be formed should the amendment be adopted ; it was leaving the work of the many to a few who would have no power to frame a constitution, but who would merely submit such suggestions for the framing of that constitution to the assembled members of the church, those members accepting or rejecting such suggestions as they considered desirable or otherwise.

Mr. Hall enquired whether legal advice had been taken by the Bishop and the gentlemen who had drawn up the resolution now before the meeting, previous to their having done so.

The opinions of several legal gentlemen including Messrs. Kerr and Campbell were given, all tending in favor of the interpretation of the act as taken by Mr. Hale.

Several observations were then made by various parties in no way complimentary to the talents of Mr. Cameron in drawing up acts of Parliament, or the infallibility of his opinion.

In reply, the Bishop stated that in drawing up the resolution they had been guided by the welfare of the church at large, and by the opinion of Mr. Cameron, the gentleman who had framed and presented the Act itself.

Mr. Hale now objected to the decision of the chair, which was, as he stated, a deviation from the general rule at all meetings. He would not acknowledge that the clergy had the right of voting separately from the rest of the meeting.

Mr. Kerr, advocate, here stepped forward, on the part of five professional gentlemen present, who had requested him to express their professional view of the right of the clergy. It was only by courtesy, in their opinion, that the right is given by the meeting, and would be given on the occasion. The clergy should not arrogate to themselves the right of voting by orders, and even the authority of John Hillyard Cameron was not generally approved. Notwithstanding that gentleman's eminence, the act he had produced at the suggestion of his fellow churchmen in Toronto, was since its passage, admitted to be nothing else than a hideous absurdity.

Mr. Forsyth concurred with Mr. Hale's amendment in all things save one ; and that was the number of the committee, twelve, which he considered far too small; he could not well see how it could be named out of this large meeting.

Mr. Hale agreed to withdraw the words "by ballot," and also that the committee should consist of an equal number of Clergy and Laity, which he desired it to be understood, was his intention in originally proposing the amendment.

On the question of how the vote for the appointment of the proposed Committee was to be taken, a very animated and irregular discussion arose; the Clergy supported by the Bishop, asserting and maintaining their right to vote by orders; a procedure which it was contended would leave the Laity in a minority. This claim on their part, at the present meeting, was strongly repudiated by Messrs. Hale, Hall, Eadon, and others.

The Revd. E. W. Sewell, whose rising was greeted with the loudest applause of the day, urged, as a senior minister of the diocese, that his brethren of the clergy would on this occasion throw aside any claim they might have to vote by orders.

The Chair being again called on by Sheriff Sewell and a number of other gentlemen, to decide the point of whether the Clergy were entitled to vote by orders,

His Lordship stated that, with all deference to the attainments of the professional gentlemen who had given their opinion of the Act by which the proceedings were governed, he held to his original view of the intent of the law, and with the Honorable Mr. Cameron's written notes of his construction of it in his hands (which document the Bishop read to the meeting) he could not set aside that right.

Mr. T. W. Lloyd thought there could be no doubt that voting by orders at present would be illegal. If the Clergy were determined that they would not vote save by orders, and if the Laity would not concede that point, business could not be carried on.

Mr. Kerr, in answer to the Bishop, said decidedly that the Laity, according to the law, were not authorised to give their assent to the Clergy voting by orders.

Mr. G. Hall then addressed the meeting on the necessity of their acting with due reflection; the course pointed out by Mr. Hale and supported by Mr. Stuart, was the only true course which could be adopted, and he begged the meeting to pause and consider well every bearing of the subject before they took action upon it. The subject was a most important one ; they were met to decide on a matter which would affect not only themselves but their children after them.

The Revd. Mr. Balfour signified his opinion that the clergy holding the position of one against a thousand, no combined action would ever result, and they would be compelled altogether to withdraw.

Capt. Rhodes stated that he was the only member of his own congregation present. This assembly was only a representation of a party of the city of Quebec. He was convinced his congregation would be most reluctant to accept the decision of the present assemblage on any point. He therefore proposed an adjournment to this day two months.

The Revd. S. S. Wood, senior clergyman of the entire diocese, and a minister eminent for his talents and usefulness to the Church, here rose and begged from his very heart and soul to disclaim the shadow of a wish to override the laity, He solemnly declared that he could not sit in a meeting where there was a disposition of any one order to overrule the others. Mr. Wood hereupon left the meeting.

Prof. Thompson said that any high-handed measure carried here, would, in all probability, be not acquiesced in by the country congregations, and thus an extensive schism might arise in the church.

The Revd. Mr. Balfour deemed it strange that, after voting themselves a Synod, the meeting were yet in doubt as to whether they constituted a Synod or not.

The Revd. H. Burrage, M.A., proposed an adjournment to that day month. All the clergy around him from the country parishes were, like himself, unaccompanied by a single lay representative, and it was but just, when such important questions of detail were discussed, that the laity should have notification thereof, and opportunity to attend.

Col. Fitzgerald said that if the meeting was properly constituted when the act was adopted, why was it not constituted now ?

The Bishop gave an explanation which had been made already.

The Bishop several times left the chair as he saw no possibility of proceeding without the principle being acknowledged of the clergy having the right to vote as a separate body.

Among the speakers who evinced warmth, the Revd. Mr. Roe declared against admitting any promiscuous assemblage to assume the rights of legislative action, that had no precedent in the history of the world, in any instance, save during the French Revolution.

During the height of the discussion, it is deeply to be lamented that any portion of the lay element should have so far forgotten themselves as to have taunted the clergy with such gross language as "Church-emptiers," "Beavens" and "Fish-eaters" Repeatedly also, to the manifest disrespect of the same class towards the chair, it could not but be noticed that much needless loud conversation and shuffling, or moving about, was kept up, whenever his lordship addressed the assemblage.

The Revd. Mr. Parkin had a paper put into his hands, containing the printed names of twelve persons, as the ballot ticket of a party. The Revd. gentleman, though the proceedings were drawing to a close, reiterated the assertion that the clergy came as independent and unfettered individuals, while that paper clearly established upon whom the imputation lay of a deliberate intent to overrule the will of the meeting.

Several propositions of adjournment were made, one of which was carried to the first Wednesday in September, when his Lordship with much emotion pronounced the benediction.

AMERICAN VIEW OF THE QUEBEC SYNOD MEETING.

(From the New York Church Journal, July 14.)

The *Quebec Mercury* gives us a full account of the opening meeting to form a Diocesan Synod, under the Colonial Act. To us, who have for so many years enjoyed the power of freely legislating for ourselves in ecclesiastical matters, the crude attempts of those who are yet novices in the noble art, afford sometimes matter of wonder. We insert a long report of the first meeting of the Quebec Synod, where the Assembly finally adjourned without doing anything but adopt the Colonial Act. And the reason why they did nothing else, was because the laity would not consent that the clergy should vote as a separate order! This absurd extreme of radicalism would swamp Bishop, priests, deacons, under the vast numerical majority of lay votes. An extreme so wild as this has never, we believe, been even temporarily adopted in any diocese of these United States; nor have we ever heard of any diocese where any sane man has ever ventured to propose it. Everywhere among us, *as a matter of course*, the clergy and the laity have coordinate powers. In some dioceses the Bishop alone forms a third coordinate power, as indeed, ought always to be the case: but even where this is not expressed in the law, there is hardly a Diocese where it is not the case *in fact*.

In the present instance, the words of the Colonial Act are clear and express. The legislative power is given to "The Bishops, Clergy, and Laity, members of the United Church of England and Ireland." They are mentioned distinctly, as being *distinct Orders*, and in their action, the consent of the *whole three* is requisite, otherwise it is no action at all. "The Bishops, Clergy, and Laity," says the act, "may *meet* and *frame constitutions* and *make regulations*," &c. If when they "*meet*," there be no "laity" there, it is evident that no business can be transacted; and no other construction than this would be tolerated by the laity themselves. By the same reasoning, the presence of the '*Bishops*' and the '*Clergy*' is equally indispensable to a valid "*meeting*" of the Body. But if this be so as to the "*meeting*," it is equally so as to the "*framing of constitutions*" and the "*making of regulations*." The same use of the same phrase settles both points in one stroke. Hence in the transaction of business, if the *laity* oppose a measure, it is not the work of the "Bishops, Clergy, and *Laity*," therefore it is nothing. If the *clergy* do not agree to it, it is not the work of "Bishops, *clergy*, and Laity; therefore it is nothing. If the *Bishops* refuse their sanction, it is not the work of the "*Bishops*, Clergy and Laity;" therefore it is nothing. So long as each of the three is distinctly recognized in the law, they *must each* have distinctive rights in all action under the law.

What makes this clearer, is, that precisely the same language is used in the second section, concerning the *Provincial* Assembly, as in the first section concerning the Diocesan Synod. This Provincial Assembly would be a body corresponding with our General Convention. And when the several Bishops of the Province come together, shall it be said that the whole Episcopate and the representatives of the whole of the Clergy, shall be over-ridden completely by a numerical superiority of laymen?

It is in admirable keeping, that those who advocate such a wild extreme of radicalism as this, should be found, in debate, to taunt the clergy with gross and insulting language, and to *shuffle* the aged and venerable Bishop, whenever he addressed the meeting. Shame ! Such a course befits such a cause, indeed ; but the sober second thought of the laity themselves will destroy every chance of success for a notion, which, if successful would—*with laity of such a temper*—soon destroy the Church. The Bishop and his Clergy did nobly well in bearing kindly and patiently with the insulting treatment they received, and yet standing firmly to the clear rights of their Orders. The Bishop *at present*, and until the adoption of a Constitution, concentrates all the ecclesiastical power of the Diocese in his own hands : and there it will be likely to remain, and *ought* to remain, until the laity are willing to render to others that fairness and justice which in this whole matter of Synodical action, which the Bishops and Clergy are so careful and so happy to concede to the laity. We doubt not that " Apostles, and elders, and brethren" will agree harmoniously and courteously on the 1st Wednesday in September.

(From the New York Church Journal, 11th Aug., 1858.)

QUEBEC, July 28, 1858.

MESSRS. EDITORS :—Having observed, in a recent number of your paper, an account of the proceedings of a meeting held in this city last month, with some editorial remarks upon them, I am prompted, in justice to this Diocese, to crave your permission to offer a few observations, with the view of setting some points in the right light before persons at a distance, who, from ignorance of the real state of the case, may be led to form very erroneous impressions. You are aware that it is now several years since a movement originated *with the Bishops* of several Colonial Dioceses for procuring the co-operation, not of their clergy only, but also of the laity, by means of synodical action, and divesting themselves of some degree of ill-defined power and painful responsibility in the management of ecclesiastical affairs. The same obstacles which stand in the way of the freedom of action of our Mother Church in this behalf, were supposed to beset us in the Colonies, and different plans were devised, and measures introduced at different periods into the Imperial and some Colonial Legislatures, for our relief. That relief was finally afforded to us in this Colony by means of the following steps :—

1. A resolution adopted by the Legislature to address the Queen on our behalf, for the passing of an Imperial Act to declare that the Colonies were not affected by the statutes which impede the action of the Church at Home ; and an address from both houses of Parliament, founded on the resolution.

2. An Address to the Crown, on the same subject, from the Canadian Bishops, forwarded and recommended by the Governor General.

3. The Home Government, being advised that difficulties lay in the way of imperial legislation on the subject, authorized and recommended the Governor General of Canada to procure the passing of an act by the Colonial Legislature empowering the Bishops, Clergy, and Laity " to form representative bodies," and giving to *such bodies* the right to frame constitutions, and, generally, to exercise the functions of Synods.

4. A Bill was accordingly brought in, not by the Government, but by an independent member, the Hon. J. Hillyard Cameron, and having been passed without difficulty, became law on the proclamation of Her Majesty's assent in 1857.

The Bishop of Toronto had anticipated the action of the Legislature, and assembled his Synod, calling together his clergy and *lay delegates.* His Synod was in session at the time that the bill was introduced into the Provincial Parliament and with the view of throwing the weight of the influence of the Synod into the scale, his lordship, followed by his clergy and *lay delegates*, made his appearance in the House of Assembly. In this Diocese it was thought better to wait the issue of legislation on the subject, and in the Autumn of last year, the clergy and lay delegates, to be chosen by every parish, mission, or chapelry, were summoned to meet in June, 1858. As the time of election of delegates drew near, it was made to appear that, according to the view taken by some legal authorities of the *literal wording* of the Act, the Bishop could not proceed without summoning, in the first instance, *all* the laity of the Diocese ; a proceeding so manifestly absurd and impracticable, that if adopted it must be only *pro formâ*, to satisfy the real or supposed requirements of the Act. The Bishop of the newly constituted Diocese of Huron had, as a measure of safety, followed this course. At the meeting in that Diocese, certain preliminary resolutions were passed, providing for the representation of the laity, "pending the adoption of a Constitution by the Synod itself." The Bishop of Quebec having deter mined to do the same, although his own conviction of the legality and correctness of his original course was unchanged, revoked the summons to the Synod, and called, instead, a pre liminary meeting of the clergy and *laity*, for the purposes of adopting the Act and making provision for the representation of the laity. Not a word was heard of objection to this course. Every thing went on smoothly. Every one understood that a meeting of a few laymen of Quebec could not be supposed to represent the Diocese, and that the business of the meeting would be simply and formally disposed of, as had been done in Huron. No one was specially invited to come, and many of the clergy were excused from undertaking a journey which would involve needless inconvenience and expense. But there were some parties who thought they had discovered even more than had been supposed in the Act : *they* beat up for recruits, organized an opposition, and the result was the disgraceful pro- ceedings which you have already chronicled. If the case of any other than merely formal action had been contemplated, measures would of course have been taken for admitting none but members of the Church, and for securing the attendance of well-affected people. But, as it was, there was but a small attendance of true Churchmen, and there were no means of ascertaining the qualification of voters, the *public*, in point of fact, being admitted, though the members of the Church of England only were invited. One minister of the Wesleyans was certainly counted among the voters ; and one gentleman *seconded a resolution* at this meeting, as well as at another of which I shall speak presently, who declared *upon oath*, not many years ago, that he considered himself as belonging to *no Church*. There were others who took a prominent part in the proceedings, whose claims to membership would certainly bear very little sifting : and some who habitually forsake the assem- bling of the saints together for public worship, but were not ashamed to take a prominent part in what ought to have been religious proceedings. It would be most unjust, therefore, to this Diocese, to take this meeting as a sample of its state of feeling. I wish it were possible for " all" its members to be together " in one place" ; for I do not hesitate to affirm that, in such a case, few dioceses would present an assemblage

where both clergy and laity would be more " of one accord."
But in a diocese of the extent of this, with settlements extreme-
ly poor and widely scattered, from the Gulf to the frontier of
Vermont, with extraordinary impediments to quick or convenient travelling, it would be of course impossible to obtain
anything like an approximation to a fair representation of its
whole laity, if *all* the dwellers in any one place were permitted
to come together and outvote the rest of the Diocese.

But I must not be tedious. I have been led into these
details from a desire to do justice to our Diocese. Up to this
point, the absolute necessity of providing for the *representation*
of the laity had apparently been taken for granted by all parties.
It was only in consequence of a real or supposed defect in the
wording of the Act that it became necessary to convene the
laity at large. No one had disputed the *intention* of the
legislature : in fact, the wisdom of the gentleman who drew
the bill, and, by necessary implication, of the Legislature
which passed it, was called in question in no very courteous
manner, for not specially providing for this point. As the
Act stood, and as we had come under its protection, we must
be careful to conform exactly to it, lest we should lose the
benefit of that protection. But now it is made all at once to
appear that the Act is not enabling, but enacting ; not reliev-
ing us from disabilities, but creating new rights. So many
wonderful notions, so many new ideas, are started, that the
Bishop, determined to be fortified by good legal advice, that he
might steer clear of all difficulties on the 1st of September (the
day fixed for the adjourned meeting), undertakes a journey to
the seat of government for the purpose of procuring the opinion
of the law officers of the Crown on certain points. The objections taken were some of them so absurd, and the *intention* of
the Legislature was so plain and so well known, that while
the Bishop was in Toronto, it was suggested by influential
persons in two different dioceses, that the simplest way of
getting rid of all the difficulties of the case would be to apply
to the Legislature for a short explanatory Act. This was
accordingly undertaken by some friends of the Church in
Toronto ; for the whole Canadian Church is involved, inasmuch as, if the view held by certain of our lawyers is established, the proceedings already had in Toronto and Huron have
been irregular and invalid. The bill passes the Legislative Coun-

c

cil, when our friends here conceive an alarm, and initiate a course of proceedings, the first step in which is to cause the editor of a *Wesleyan* paper to " understand" that the Bishop had put measures in train for passing the Bill before leaving Quebec, and then undertaken the journey, and despatched the business quietly, " or, as some think, *clandestinely.*" The liberties of the people are in danger ; the laity of the Diocese have been betrayed by him who has been their Bishop for twenty-two years, and has gone in and out among the people of Quebec as their Rector for nearly twice that length of time. On the strength of this anonymous *understanding*, a public meeting must be called, vehement indignation expressed, the perfidy of the Bishop denounced, and the bill stopped ! Unfortunately for those interested, it becomes known that the " understanding" is directly opposed to the " facts" of the case. The public meeting, notwithstanding, proceeds—called by anonymous placards, it is avoided by intelligent Churchmen with scarcely an exception.

It included a large number of persons not belonging to the Church—and a reference to the resolutions (*) will shew what manner of spirit *they* are of, who while they promise liberty to the Churchmen of Quebec, would disfranchise six sevenths of the Diocese, and while they make their boast of enlightenment, intelligence, and justice, would establish the principle that the *Episcopal* Church is to be governed, not even by Bishops, Clergy, and Lay Representatives—nor yet by Bishops, clergy, and *laity at large*, acting in concert, in their several orders, but by an indiscriminate majority of such a body—in other words, by a majority of the laity in any one town where the Synod might happen to meet !

This is the body that is to exercise all the powers conferred by the act—of *enforcing discipline*—appointing to, or *removing from*, ecclesiastical offices of *whatever grade*, &c. ! !

I am truly sorry to have intruded at such length upon your space, and I will now conclude with mentioning two points, which help to throw light on the consistency and fairness of these proceedings. 1. The honorable gentleman (a sincere friend of the Church) who introduced into the Legislature the

(*) See Report of Proceedings, in Appendix (A) to Address of Lay Association, p.p., 7,8.

measures so fraught with danger to the laity— though he no
doubt thought it would commend itself to all reasonable men—
was the same who in the Synod, held last month at Toronto,
seconded the proposal for abolishing the Episcopal veto. Yet
even his name was not a sufficient protection. He will be
surprised probably to find himself " insidiously" curtailing the
rights of the *laity !* I shall be much surprised if he does not
now see the need of the *veto.* 2. The Act of 1856 was passed by a Legislature neither professing, nor expected, to know
anything of the Constitution of the Church, but with the actual
living reality of a Church Synod before their eyes at the time,
in their own House. They supposed, in the innocence of
their hearts, that they were simply performing an act of justice
in declaring it lawful for *such a body* to meet in Synod—they
called *this body* the **Bishops,** *clergy and laity* : and having
set them free from doubts and disabilities, and so done *all* that
they intended, or were asked to do, they parted company with
them, in hope to meet no more,—in which hope I am afraid
some of your readers, and perhaps yourself, will part with
your faithful servant.

M. A.

(*From the Quebec Mercury, July 29.*)

At the meeting held on Monday evening in the Court
House in connection with the establishment of a diocesan
Synod, the resolutions proposed were (as we have stated) passed
without any opposition. In fairness we should have added
that it could not well be otherwise, for the meeting was got
up by parties of the same way of thinking ; and as it had not
been announced by whom the meeting was called together,
whether by churchmen or by dissenters, few members of the
Anglican Church, who usually take an interest in public
demonstrations of the kind, were present. Mr. Okill Stuart
alone raised his voice against the imprudent and unadvisable
nature of the proceedings. Mr. Cameron's Act had been found
defective and impracticable in Upper Canada as well as in this
diocese, and hence an amended Act had become requisite. All
persons sincerely desiring to see a Synod established in a har-

monious and becoming manner, consistent too with the working of the British constitution, would do well to avoid throwing any impediments in the way so as to obstruct the passing of the new bill, which has already passed through the Upper House. The Bill does not attempt to determine what the constitution of the Diocesan Synod shall be; but merely defines how the members of the Church shall meet by representation to decide upon that point, and other initiatory matters. The preliminary meeting in the National School House, it has been observed, bore no inconsiderable resemblance to the famous Council at Ephesus, both for virulence of language and violence of conduct. There was, however, an important difference. At Ephesus the members of the Synod actually came to blows; in Quebec we certainly were more moderate. We must confess that we do not think that a meeting convened in the manner of the Quebec Synodical meeting could transact business satisfactorily. Mass meetings of any kind are contrary both to the spirit and practice of the British constitution. However well they may be adapted for republican, they certainly are not consistent with monarchical institutions. It has always been a principle among British subjects that the people are properly represented by representatives chosen by the people themselves. Mr. Cameron, the framer of the Synodical Bill, evidently had this principle in view when he framed the Bill: he has since admitted this. It is absurd to suppose that the Church of England in the Diocese of Quebec can be represented by a meeting in Quebec, consisting chiefly of Quebec people, and in which persons take a prominent part, who are not even members of the Church of England. People in Quebec would think it very unjust if such a meeting were convened at Three Rivers, or at Sherbrooke. The natural conclusion then is, that a Synodical mass-meeting in Quebec, is a great injustice to the members of the Church in the diocese, who live at a distance from Quebec.

Representatives properly chosen from each church or mission, is the obvious remedy for the defects at which we have hinted. Eminent lawyers seem to have doubts about the legality of a meeting so assembled, although Mr. Cameron has stated that the Synodical Bill was expressly framed with that object in view. There are few great questions on which eminent lawyers do not hold different opinions. They are so accustomed to split hairs into filaments, and filaments into shreds, and to twist and bend the matter before them, that differences and distinctions are sure to arise upon every question which is discussed. But such hair-splitting and dilly-dallying ought not to be practised by men, who do not found their opinions upon nice legal distinctions, but upon broad general principles. If every member of the Church in the Diocese were to come to such a meeting, what room in Quebec would be large enough to hold them? What business could possibly be transacted in such an assemblage? There would be a perpetual virtual adjournment, and perhaps, after the lapse of some centuries by some fortunate circumstance a Synod might be established.

(From the Quebec Morning Chronicle, July 29, 1858.)

We publish, to-day, the new Bill brought before the Provincial Legislature, for the purpose of facilitating the means of establishing Synods of the Anglican Church in the several dioceses of the Province. We annex also a copy of the petition, which has been forwarded in favor of the said Bill; the signatures, we understand, were got up in a few hours, and might have been with ease many times multiplied. That Mr. Cameron's Act, interpreted (as some of our Quebec lawyers are disposed to do) according to the letter and not the spirit, would prove impracticable, and be applied in a manner totally at variance with British constitutional action, was a circumstance foreseen and predicted by many. The correctness of such sentiments was explained and maintained in a leading article of this journal immediately after the abortive proceedings at the late noisy preliminary meeting, held in the National School-house. Professed attempts to convoke the assemblage of a whole nation, province or diocese, in one city or on one vast plain, may suit republican bombast, or serve to gratify the unlicensed will and policy of a despot. Constitutional usage has disclaimed such practices; and the people, now-a-days, assemble for legislative purposes in the persons of their representatives. By this means a fair and an impartial representation is secured to remote districts, as well as to places in the vicinity of head-quarters. The new Bill remedies the alleged inconsistencies of Mr. Cameron's Act in this respect ; and will appear to all moderate and practical persons abundantly liberal in its details. This is the result, moreover, of the best opinions that could be collected on the subject conjointly with the Dioceses of Upper Canada; but the bill and the petition speak for themselves.—With regard to the meeting, held on Monday evening, in the Court House, a brief and candid statement of the proceedings was given in the Chronicle of Tuesday ; and it was perfectly well understood that the resolutions were passed there and then with such unanimity, because the meeting consisted only of those who appear to unite in taking an opposite view of the matter and a few other persons of various denominations attending from motives of curiosity. In the announcement that such a meeting was to be held, it was not stated by whom it was called ; and most of the leading members of the Episcopal community, who are usually present at public meetings connected with the interests of the Church, declined for that reason to attend. Mr. Okill Stuart, who entered fortuitously for the purpose of introducing a friend from Kingston, was the only person who spoke against the course of proceedings ; and he could not avoid deprecating the obstructions, which were being perhaps undesignedly made to impede the passage of the explanatory and amended Bill, introduced for the purpose of removing difficulties, and of clearing the way towards the establishment of Synodical action in the different dioceses on a sound and legal basis.--There has been much misapprehension in this matter, and consequently much heat and excitement have followed ; but, really now, cannot the members of the Church of England in this city, for once in a way, with so important and solemn an object in view, agree to sink minor differences of opinion, to avoid disputes on mere technicalities, and to combine their exertions in securing an effective and a properly constituted synod ?

An Act to explain and amend the Act intituled " Act to enable " the Members of the United Church of England and Ire-" land in Canada, to meet in Synod."

Whereas doubts exist whether in the Act passed in the Session held in the nineteenth and twentieth years of Her Majesty's Reign, intituled, " An Act to enable the Members " of the United Church of England and Ireland in Canada, to

" meet in Synod," sufficient provision is made for the representation of the Laity of the United Church of England and Ireland in the Synods by the said Act authorized to be held, and it is expedient that such doubts should be removed : Therefore, Her Majesty, by and with the advice and consent of the Legislative Council and Assembly of Canada, enacts as follows :

1. For all the purposes of the aforesaid Act, the Laity shall meet by representation ; and until it shall be otherwise determined by the Synod in each Diocese, one or more delegates (not exceeding three in any case,) may be elected at the annual Easter meetings in each parish, *mission or cure within the diocese, or in cases where there may be more than one congregation in any parish mission or cure, then each such congregation,* or at a meeting to be specially called for the purpose by each Clergyman having a separate cure of souls ; and all laymen within such *parish, mission or cure or belonging to such congregation,* of the full age of twenty-one years, who shall declare themselves, in writing, at such meetings, to be members of the United Church of England and Ireland, and to belong to no other religious denomination, should have the right of voting at such election. Each delegate shall receive from the Chairman of the meeting a certificate of his election, which he shall produce, when called upon so to do, at the Synod ; and the first meeting of such Synod shall be called by the Bishop of the Diocese at such time and place as he shall think fit ; Provided always, that no business shall be transacted by the Synod of any Diocese unless at least one fourth of the Clergy of such Diocese shall be present, and at least one fourth of the Congregations within the same be represented by at least one delegate.

2. All proceedings heretofore had in any Diocese under the aforesaid Act, which have been comformable to the provisions of this Act, shall be held to be valid, as if the same had taken place after the passing of this Act. (*)

The following is a copy of the Petition forwarded to the Legislature from members of the Anglican Church, residing in Quebec, in favor of the foregoing explanatory Act relating to the formation of Synods in the several dioceses of the Province :—

(*) The Act is here printed as it actually passed, with amendments, not as it appeared in the *Chronicle* of 29th July. The amendments are in italics.

That doubts having been raised as to the meaning of the Act, &c., it is just and expedient that such doubts should be removed.

That it is held in some quarters, that no action can be taken under the said Act unless by a meeting of the Bishop, Clergy and Laity of a Diocese at large.

That it is manifestly impossible to assemble the whole of the laity of a Diocese in any one place except by representation : and that to summon them otherwise would be an act of unfairness to the members to the Church in all other portions of the Diocese, who would virtually be excluded from any share in the proceedings.

That the intention of the Legislature in passing the said Act may fairly be presumed to have been, not to introduce a system which it is impossible to carry out, and for which no precedent whatever can be found, but simply to relieve the members of the Church of England from certain disabilities under which they were supposed to lie, and to afford such relief by legalizing such synods as were fully known to have been held in the city of Toronto, before the passing of the said Act, in which the laity acted by their representatives.

That such intention was universally assumed and acted upon in the Diocese of Toronto, containing at least five-sixths of the members of the Church of England within this Province.

That your petitioners have no hesitation in expressing their firm conviction that they represent the wishes and feelings of the vast majority of the members of the Church within this Diocese.

Therefore your petitioners humbly pray that your honorable House would be pleased to pass an act to explain the intention of the Legislature in this particular.

Signed by G. J. Quebec, John B. Parkin, W. Andrew, M. A., Fredk. Andrews, H. Black, G. Okill Stuart, G. Pemberton, J. M. Fraser, J. Bell Forsyth, J. W. Dunscomb, Henry Burstall, Wm. Petry, Wm. Price, R. H. Smith, H. Pemberton, Ed. Burstall, A. D. Bell, Armine W. Mountain, E, C. Parkin, J. Magill, G. A. Wood, W. G. Petry, C. Hamilton, W. H. Anderson, H. LeMesurier, Jr., W. Rhodes, C. R. O'Connor, B. Cole, H. G. Forsyth, C. N. Montizambert, H. Kirwin, H. Petry, Clk., W. H. Tilstone, H. May, C. H. E. Tilstone, &c , &c., &c,

(*From the Quebec Morning Chronicle, July 30, 1858.*)

We have been charged by a correspondent with unfairness in having omitted certain words in the copy of the new Bill for the establishment of Synods, which appeared in yesterday's *Chronicle*. We were very anxious to ascertain what unfortunate omission had been made, and on applying to our correspondent, we found out that three or four words had been accidentally omitted, which words our correspondent thought of great importance. Fortunately we find the meaning is complete without them; but the words were in the printed copy given to be set up, and as the document reads correctly without them, the omission escaped notice in the correction of the Press.

The sentence runs thus, the words omitted being italicised : " One or more delegates (not exceeding three in any case) may be elected at the annual Easter meetings *in each Parish, or at meetings* to be specially called for the purpose by each clergyman having a separate cure of souls." The meaning manifestly is that every cure in the diocese will have the privilege of sending lay delegates, and the word parish is actually inapplicable for general purpose in the Anglican diocese of Quebec ; perhaps the word ' missions ' might have been introduced, but the word ' cure ' is of more general application and includes both parishes and missions, as well as regularly organised congregations under ministers of their own. While on this subject, we should wish to take the opportunity of alluding to the report, which appeared in a cotemporary, of Mr. Okill Stuart's speech at the meeting held in the Court House on Monday evening. The report says that Mr. Stuart spoke at great length on representation by delegation, which (he maintained) was capable of producing all necessary effects. Now this portion of his remarks would seem almost designedly to have been kept back, inasmuch as it received, and could receive no satisfactory answer. It is quite obvious that in a diocese extending from the entrance of the Gulf of St. Lawrence to the confines of Vermont, covering immense territories, unless some system be adopted to enable remote missions to be represented at any Synodical meeting held in Quebec, the members of the Church of England in those remote districts would be in a manner wholly excluded from taking part in the so much lauded self-government. The effect, in truth, would be to throw into the hands of the section, so actively engaged in resisting a measure intended for the general benefit of the church, the whole Synodical control, which the parties, who conducted the meeting of Monday evening, are evidently desirous of concentrating in themselves here in Quebec. The Bill before the House removes the difficulties and disabilities, which would press unfairly on all the members of the church at any distance from the city, and enables them to send repre-sentatives chosen by themselves to attend to their interests. The number of clergy, licensed to cures in the diocese by the Bishop, amounts to something like forty; if the laity are anxious and zealous in the matter their numbers in the preli-minary or initiative meetings of Synod may triply exceed those of the clergy. The new Bill, as Mr. Stuart clearly shewed, greatly surpasses in liberality and distinctness the provisions of the Act, which it explains and amends.

(From the Quebec Morning Chronicle, Aug. 17, 1858.)

The Bill explaining and amending the Act passed last year, to enable the members of the Anglican Church in Canada to meet in Synod has now became law. As this explanatory Act was framed partly in deference to the opinions and scruples of persons in Quebec, and for the general purpose of removing doubts " whether sufficient provision was made for the representation of the laity in the Synods authorised by the previous Act to be held;" it is now to be hoped, that no further obstructions will prevent the establish-ment of Synodical action in this diocese. It would perhaps tend to promote more amicable feelings and greater unanimity in the course of future proceedings, if a clear understanding prevailed respecting the genuine facts of the matter on some points, which are likely to excite distrust and difference of opinion. The question of voting by orders, and the so-called right of veto claimed on the part of the Bi-shop have been cited as topics of such a nature, calling for explanation. These two items, however, only present two different phases of the same question. It is, we believe, universally admitted that Synods of the Episcopalian Reformed Church should consist of three different orders: " The Bishop, the Presbyters or other Clergy of the diocese in Priests' orders, and Representatives of the Laity." At any rate the dioceses in Canada West, and the colonial dioceses of Melbourne, Adelaide, New Zealand, &c., &c., have all independently arrived at this conclusion; and have placed these three orders reciprocally on an equal footing, so that their concurrent consent, or an actual majority in each order, is requisite for carrying any measure. On the meeting of Synod the Clergy and Laity are assembled together in the same apartment, and the Bishop, if present, presides. And thus they may continue to deliberate, act and vote together, as is usually done in any other ordinary meetings. But should any clerical or lay member perceive that there is a decided majority of his own order against a measure, favorably received by the conjoint assembly, he may demand that the votes be taken by orders, and in that case unless there is an actual majority in each order, the measure cannot be pressed.—Hence it may arise, that when only one Bishop is present (as must generally be the case in diocesan synods) if he cannot conscientiously assent to the joint determination of the Presbyters and the Laity, and refuses to concur, then, by withholding his consent, he not only appears in possession of, but in the act of exercising the Veto power. It is manifest, however, that the Presbyters and the Laity respectively possess the same privilege and power as entirely as the Bishop, who represents in the Synod the Episcopal order. There is in such an institution an evident imitation of the monarchical and constitutional system of government. To withhold the Episcopal consent, like the refusal of the Royal sanction would be a negative, not an active power, and the exercise of such would soon be found to be as rare as it would certainly become dangerous and impracticable. In the United States, where the model will naturally follow the republican rather than the monarchical practice, this negative power is generally limited on the part of the Bishop, so that he must give way, if the same measure is brought up after the repeated approval of the other two orders. But the Bishop and his clergy are not likely to differ very perseveringly, and less likely to conspire against the laity. In the States the Bishop has also the power of appealing to the general synod of Bishops, who can thus restrain the effects of any local agitation, and prevent any violent and partial changes in the discipline or ruling principles of the Church. There is not yet any general Episcopal synod in this country, and until there will be, the question may stand over. But indeed these points and any other debateable matters must be practically taken into consideration, when the conventional synod meets, and the proper steps are pursued to draw up a constitution and canons for future direction and guidance. A very respectable gentleman of New York, in discussing the advantages of synodal action with a friend from Canada, said: that the system was one of the few safeguards of conservatism left in the States, and worked effectively;

that the laity never sought to over-reach or overwhelm the influence and power of the clergy ; they thought that church matters were likely to be best managed by persons professionally educated and professionally connected with them. Of course when called upon to assist in temporalities, the laymen of the church acted with zeal and liberality, nor would they neglect their duty in resisting useless innovations and in maintaining the conservative principles and character of their beloved and respected ecclesiastical institutions.

(From the Quebec Mercury, August 19, 1858.)

In connection with the subject of Synodical action on the part of the Members of the Church of England, we publish the following diocesan circular just issued to his clergy by the Lord Bishop of Quebec.

(CIRCULAR.)

BARDFIELD, NEAR QUEBEC,
18th August, 1858.

REV. AND DEAR SIR,

You are aware that, in consequence of a particular construction put upon the first clause of the enabling Act relative to Synodical powers, I was induced, after full consultation with persons competent to give advice in Church affairs, to revoke my Circular of the 25th of September, 1857, summoning the Clergy and the Lay-delegates, for whose election provision had been made, to meet at Quebec, on the 9th of June last ; and to issue another, summoning a meeting to be held upon a different principle, on the 24th of that month.

You are also aware that the reason for this postponement was not that I had any misgiving in my own mind respecting the propriety or the legality of the step which had been taken, but that we might proceed to our task without being liable to be called in question upon a point of law on which different opinions were held, and that the initiation of our Synodical proceedings, might rest, in the eyes of all men, upon a well-assured basis.

The construction to which I have referred, of the Act in question, imports the necessity of calling together the members of the Church throughout the Diocese,—that is to say, of calling together at Quebec or some one other place, all the members of the Church scattered here and there, chiefly in poor settlements and with wretchedly imperfect facilities for travelling, from the Magdalen Islands to Stanstead,—the Church of England population at Quebec, constituting, so far as is ascertainable, perhaps not more than one sixth of the whole number.

As it is evident upon the very first aspect of the case, that even a remote approximation to any expressed sense of the Diocese, could not, by possibility, be arrived at in a meeting so called, I took it for granted that, in common good faith, the meeting could only be regarded as a *pro forma* proceeding to satisfy the real or supposed requirements of the Law; and having conferred and concerted arrangements with gentlemen of different sentiments upon Church questions who all seemed to regard the matter in the same light, I went down to the meeting with no other preparation than that which enabled us to propose to its consideration the simple Resolutions already adopted in the correspondent case of the Diocese of Huron, which were essential for setting the machinery of the Synod in motion.

I shall not here enter into any description of what took place at the Meeting when assembled. Whatever notice my duty may impose it upon me to take of that unhappy scene, I reserve to be given, D. V., in another form. Suffice it to say that an adjournment took place to the 1st of September : but not before it had become apparent that great confusion and multiplied mischiefs must ensue from the Act as interpreted to require a meeting of the members of the Church otherwise than by representation, as well as that extraordinary prejudice must thence done to the rights of the Diocese at large.

A Bill was subsequently introduced into the Provincial Parliament through the intervention of some leading laymen in different Dioceses of the Province, for the remedy of these evils and the relief of the Church, which Bill having become Law, the aforesaid adjourned Meeting of necessity falls through; and you will consequently be pleased to notify your Congregation or Congregations that no such adjourned Meeting will take place. (†) The Meeting on St. John the Baptist's day, was *called* for *two* objects : 1stly, the adoption of the Act, 2ndly, the establishment of the principle of representation :— the former was disposed of upon the occasion :—the latter has been provided for by the Legislature, and so far as the Laity are concerned, any other mode of meeting than by representation is made illegal.

I cannot close this Circular without expressing my warm and

---

† The passing of the Bill (and I speak under advice) is by no means the *only* ground for setting aside the adjourned meeting ; but it is of itself, a proper and sufficient ground.

thankful appreciation of the unanimous assurance, communicated to me after the scene of the 24th of June, in the shape of a resolution passed by a large meeting of Clergymen, of their attachment to my person, and their confidence in my administration of the Diocese. It was indeed a great comfort to my heart--next to the hope of the Divine approval in the consciousness of acting with a single eye to the glory of God, the good of His Church, and the salvation of souls through Christ, the greatest comfort in these times of disturbance, which I can possibly enjoy.

I am,

Dear Sir,

Your affectionate Brother in Christ,

G. J. QUEBEC.

(From the Quebec Mercury, August 31, 1858.)

The Lord Bishop of Quebec, returned to town on Saturday morning, and on the afternoon of the same day left town again for Sherbrooke, having been solicited to attend the reopening of the Church of that place which has been for some time undergoing repairs. On Sunday morning before service he was greeted by the assembled congregation with the subjoined address, signed by the body of pewholders, which was read by R. W. Heneker, Esqr., one of the Church Wardens :—

To the Right Revd. the Lord Bishop of Quebec.

We, the parishioners of St. Peter's Church, Sherbrooke, desire to express to your Lordship the very great gratification we feel at your Lordship's kind visit to us on this, the occasion of re-opening of our Church for Divine Service.

We beg to assure your Lordship that, apart from the reverence due to your high office, we entertain for you, personally, the strongest feelings of regard :—feelings, we are bound to say, due to the kindly sympathy you have at all times displayed in our affairs.

We are conscious that in your high position, great responsibility must of necessity entail great anxiety, and if the attached feelings of a humble branch of the Church in your diocese can in any measure alleviate that anxiety, we tender you with all respect, such attachment.

In conclusion, we trust that you may long be spared to guide the Church of this Diocese, into that position befitting the Church of Christ, when (under the action of self-government recently granted to us), remedies may be found for all internal troubles, and we may shew to the world that free discussion and harmonious action may be co-existent.

Signed by

R. W. Heneker, ⎱
Alex. Winter, ⎰ Churchwardens.
and fifty-four others.

His Lordship replied as follows :—

My Christian Brethren :—The very kind address which you have taken the occasion of my visit to present to me, is the more gratifying to my feelings because it was entirely unexpected.

In the relation in which it has pleased God that I should stand to you, the assurances of your attachment and your confidence would, at any time, be precious to me ; for although I have never, as I trust, made it my object to seek the praise of men, yet it is a happy and soothing encouragement in the labours of the Ministry, to gain the affection and respect of a Christian flock, and the prominence in the Diocese, of this particular charge, gives weight to the testimony of the congregation.

The difficulties and obstructions with which the Church of England has to contend in planting her institutions and providing for the immediate wants of her people in a Diocese like this, do indeed present grounds for anxiety which, if the cause were not in higher hands than those of man, might prompt us to despair ; and the responsibilities attaching to the administration of such a Diocese, are often harrassing in the extreme. Conscious in the execution of such a task, that we are but " earthen vessels" and distrustful of our own wisdom at every step, we can only say that " Seeing we have this Ministry, as we have received mercy, we faint not," for our sufficiency is in Christ. And so long as we can conscientiously say to our lay brethren, in the maintenance, for the common benefit, of what we conceive to be safe and primitive principles, that " we preach not ourselves but Christ Jesus the Lord and ourselves their servants for Jesus' sake," we claim their indulgent judgment, as we are gratified by their appreciation of our faithfulness.

For whatever little time it may please God that I should " abide in the flesh," (to be succeeded, as I pray, by some one who will more ably fill the charge,) the Laity of the Diocese at large will, I am persuaded, do me the same justice, in their estimate of my fidelity to their interests, which has been rendered by yourselves; and most cordially do I respond to the hope and happy anticipation which you express, that the cooperation of the laity which we of the episcopal order, have invited and have used long and at last successful endeavors to put in train, may be, as the experiment proceeds, carried on in this as it is already in so many other Colonial Dioceses, at once with full advantage to the Church and with harmonious understanding between its different orders, in their united work.

I will only add,—with reference to the occasion which brought me here,—that I am thankful to witness the improvements in your Church, and I fervently pray that the words applied by the patriarch to the solitary spot which he consecrated as having there held Communion with the Almighty may, in their best sense, be verified to your experience, within these walls.—This is none other than the house of God, and this is the gate of heaven.

(*From the Quebec Mercury, 4th September*, 1858.)

Our contemporary the *Gazette* has for some weeks teemed with articles, squibs, &c., upon Synodical action. In a recent number (August 30th) the Editorial WE was used in a strange not to say singular manner. The writer represented himself as standing upon the vantage ground of Truth and calmly and complacently surveying the errors, wanderings and mists, in the vale of Synodical action below.

A Methodist, he naturally, though by no means logically assumes that Methodism, the eminence on which he has taken his stand, is the Hill of Truth. Professing neutrality, he seems to forget that his paper bears tri-weekly proof that he is a violent partizan ; that, like many moralists, his preaching and his practice are totally dissimilar.

Without wishing to offer the slightest offence to the respectable sect of Methodists, we may be allowed to doubt whether a Methodist is better able to judge of the affairs of the Church of England than the members of that Church. We wish it to be particularly understood that we have not the remotest desire to quarrel with the peculiar tastes of any Sect. But our excellent contemporary must forgive us for not wishing to see the Clergy of our Church, as an Order, swamped, and the Bishop reduced to a nullity.

The Act to amend the Act for Synodical meetings, &c., which has now become law is sufficiently liberal in its terms to satisfy every layman who is really a member of the Church of England. The most liberal measures have been taken to ensure the due representation of the laity at the forthcoming meeting. Each congregation chooses as its delegates those who most possess its confidence ; the congregation will therefore have itself to blame if it selects unworthy representatives. The meeting, besides, is but a preliminary meeting in which all points connected with Synodical action, from the veto downwards, must be discussed and arranged. It seems probable that members of the Church of England in this Province will have more confidence in a meeting composed of delegates, duly chosen by members of the Church, than in a mass meeting consisting of a variety of sects, in which any one could pour forth at will his views and his venom. The recently passed act to amend the act for Synodical meetings, &c., will certainly prevent the recurrence of those disgraceful scenes which took place at the meeting in the National School House. This, perhaps, may render it unpopular with certain people who have a morbid predilection for such stormy reunions. But the great majority of the laity will, we feel satisfied, be glad that the measures for the government of the Church will be discussed and arranged with calmness and deliberation, not amid the tumult and uproar of a heterogeneous mob.

(*From the Church Journal, Oct.* 13, 1858.)

THE SYMPATHISERS.—Our columns not long ago contained an account of a meeting in Quebec, at which the Bishop and

Clergy were treated in the most unhandsome if not insulting manner, by some who claimed to be insisting upon the "rights of the laity." The *Protestant Churchman* copies a condensed report of a second public meeting, in which are set forth the complaints and claims of this clamorous party ; and gives moreover full editorial endorsement to the faction, saying that it " cannot but sympathize in the efforts afoot for the recognition and maintenance of *lay rights* in the Canadian Church."

The first complaint made at that meeting was, that the constitution of the church in that Diocese was not to be submitted " to a general meeting of its members," instead of being acted on only by lay deputies. It this be a deprivation of *lay rights* there are no lay rights on this side of the line ; for none of our Diocesan constitutions have ever been submitted to any such " general meeting of members." They have all become law by the action of Conventions in which the laity appeared only by lay-delegates, as in all our other Church legislation.

The late Explanatory Act passed by the Provincial Parliament, is then found fault with as " unfair" and " against the will of those interested in the working of those alterations." But why ? Because " the popular principle of *representation by population* has been scouted, and the *laity of the city* almost ignored." . . . " Under the amended law, . . . Quebec *would always be in a minority.*" Calculations were given showing that the lay delegates from the country would be *much more numerous* than those from the city. Astonishing ! Does " the recognition and maintenance of lay rights" require that the *city* delegates should outnumber those from the country parishes ? Then why does not the *Protestant Churchman* commence agitating for " lay rights" here at home ? For it is precisely the same case in the Diocese of New York. Of our 274 parishes, only about 50 are in this city,—a city, too, rather larger than even Quebec. In a full Convention therefore the country would have a majority of 678 votes over the city. Yet nobody complains in New York. Why should the *Protestant Churchman* lend itself to support agitation in Quebec, on grounds which it would be ashamed to act on at home ?

But " the popular principle of representation by population has been scouted." What of it ? It is scouted here in New York as well. The smallest parish organized a few days ago in a country village, has the same lay representation in our Convention as the oldest and wealthiest parish (those only excepted which have more than one consecrated building and more than one congregation). Even country parishes so small that they cannot furnish three male communicants to be deputies, are, as the *Protestant Churchman* contends, entitled to the *right* of being represented by *non*-communicants. And here in New York, it claims that it is an *encroachment* upon " the rights of the laity" to *refuse* to such a weak little country parish, a position equal, in Convention, to that of S. George's Stuyvesant Square, with its 800 communicants. But there is no complaint here. The laity in New York are not conscious of any oppression. Why does not the *Protestant Churchman* commence the war for " lay rights" in New York ? And if there is no cause of complaint in New York, why does it sympathize with the faction in Quebec which is fighting *against* precisely the same state of things that prevails all over the Church of the United States ? Nay, it pervades our General Convention as well ; and the smallest frontier Diocese, with only six or eight clergymen, is entitled to as large a representation, and throws as heavy a vote, as this great Diocese of New York with between 300 and 400 clergy. If there be oppression in the case, therefore, we churchmen are universally oppressed here, in the United States !

When it is remembered, on the one hand, that the late Act of the Provincial Parliament against which such clamors are raised, was passed after the utmost efforts its opponents could make ; that it was passed by a mixed body of Romanists, Churchmen, Dissenters, and Nothingarians ; that it was passed by the very strong vote of *seventy-two* to *seven* ; and that every Churchman in the House voted *in favor* of it ; and when, on the other hand, it is seen that every organic point on which sympathy is expressed by the *Protestant Churchman* is in agreement with the system in universal practice among us, without serious complaint anywhere in the United States—without complaint even from the *Protestant Churchman* here at home ; it will then be understood how utterly empty are the pretexts of the faction in Quebec, and how gratuitously mischievous is the " sympathy" so cordially expressed by our contemporary. Indeed, the latter is so little creditable in any respect, that we prefer considering it as merely—an accident.

(*From the Church Journal*, Oct. 13, 1858)

DIOCESE OF HURON.

The importance of the late meeting of Synod, and the sound principles which it embodied in the Constitution of that new Diocese, induce us to give the following letter, which furnishes a rather fuller account of the proceedings than we have had before :—

Messrs. Editors :—To the notices already contained in your columns of the affairs of this young Diocese, may now be added an account of our first Diocesan Synod, which was held at London, C. W., on Tuesday and Wednesday the 21st and 22d inst. To this meeting many of the clergy had been looking forward with more than ordinary anxiety, the principal object with which it was convened being the adoption of a Constitution, which therefore involved the settlement of the principles upon which the administration of the Diocese should hereafter be conducted. This anxiety had been mainly occasioned by a draft of a Constitution, put forth some months ago, by the Committee appointed to perform this duty at a general meeting of the Clergy and Laity of the Diocese, which took place in February last. One article of the proposed Constitution—that providing for the election of lay representatives—gave the right of voting at the parochial meetings held for that purpose, not only to the actual members of each congregation, but also to " habitual worshippers in the same." This provision would evidently have extended the right of voting to Methodists and other dissenters, who in many of our more remote country parishes are frequently habitual worshippers in our congregations. And although it is not probable that many of them would have desired to avail themselves of the privilege, it was felt that the giving it them at all would be a serious violation of Church principles. Another of the proposed articles was as follows :— " No act or resolution on its first introduction shall become law without the concurrence of the Bishop and a majority of the Clergy and Laity present, provided that, ordinarily, the votes of the whole Synod shall be taken collectively ; but that at the desire of the Bishop, or at the request of five clergymen, or of five laymen, the votes of each of the above named Orders shall be taken separately ; and if any difference still subsist when such vote is so taken, then the subject under deliberation shall stand over for consideration to the ensuing Synod, and if then passed by a majority of three-fourths of the Clergy and Laity respectively, it shall be adopted." To this proposition, the objection entertained by many of the Clergy, was if possible stronger than to that previously alluded to. There was a very deep conviction on the minds of not a few, that the question at issue was in reality nothing less than Episcopacy itself ; that should the Bishop by the adoption of this Constitution, be placed in such a position as, under certain circumstances, to be deprived of his legislative functions in the Diocese, his office would be a mere sham. As the relative strength of the parties into which the Diocese was divided on this great and fundamental question, was not precisely known, the discussion was looked forward to with the more anxiety, though not without a steadfast determination to oppose to the utmost the adoption of the proposed articles.

The Clergy and Laity assembled on Tuesday morning, the 21st inst , and after attending divine service at St. Paul's Cathedral, adjourned to the adjoining schoolhouse, when the Synod was organized. The Bishop opened the proceedings by a brief statement of the various matters of interest to the Diocese which had occurred since the meeting in February, dwelling particularly on the Act of the Legislature which has been recently passed explanatory of the Synod Act of 1856, and giving an account of his late confirmation tour, in the course of which, although he has yet gone through but a portion of the Diocese, he has confirmed nearly 1,000 persons. The rules for the preservation of order which formed part of the proposed Constitution, having then been adopted, and declared to be of force for the present meeting, the business of the day commenced in earnest, with the consideration of the Constitution, the articles of which were read and discussed seriatim.

Previously to this, however, it was announced that the Committee had, before the assembling of the Synod, resolved on a modification of the Constitution they had previously put forth, and as article after article of the Constitution thus amended by them was read, it appeared that all those to which objection had been taken, had been so altered as to meet the views of the most conservative of Churchmen. Under these circumstances, of course, the happiest unanimity prevailed. Discussion was confined for the most part to matters of detail, and the constitution of the Di)cese was established, as we hope, for all time to come, on a sound and Catholic basis. The principal features of the Constitution may be expressed in a few words. Each duly organized congregation in the Diocese is to have the privilege of sending to the Synod one, two, or three Lay representatives, according to its number of registered voters. The voters are to record their names in a book as " Members of the United Church of England and Ireland," and as belonging to no other religious denomination. The lay representatives are to be communicants of at least one year's standing. The Synod is to meet annually ; this is imperative, and it was a point on which the Committee laid much stress. The article before given was amended as follows :—" No act or resolution shall become law without the concurrence of the Bishop, and a majority of the Clergy and Laity present, provided that ordinarily the votes of the last mentioned orders shall be taken collectively : but that at the desire of the Bishop, or at the request of five Clergymen, or of five Laymen,they shall be taken separately." The consideration of the Constitution occupied the Synod during the afternoon session of Tuesday, and the morning session of Wednesday. On Wednesday afternoon a very animated debate took place on a motion to address the Legislature upon the question of religious instruction in Common Schools, but although all present were unanimous as to the importance of the object, no definite plan for carrying it into effect could be agreed upon, and the motion, with a proposed amendment, was ultimately withdrawn.

With the appointment of some Committees the business of the Synod then terminated ; and all felt thankful for the important results thus so happily attained.

The evenings of Tuesday and Wednesday were devoted to the affairs of the Diocesan Church Society, which has recently received its charter of incorporation from the Provincial Legislature. The principal business in connection with this institution, also, was the adoption of a Constitution ; but in this, as in the former case, the discussion was confined to matters of detail, the Constitution drafted by the Committee having, in its principles and general features, met with general acceptance. The most important difference between the Constitution of the

Church Society of Huron, and that of the Diocese of Toronto, consists in the arrangement that all moneys collected for the Society, or any of its objects, shall be paid into the General Fund to be administered by the Standing Committee, instead of in part by the Committees of District Associations, which are in fact now merged in the general body.

Subsequently to the adoption of the Constitution, on the second evening, a question was brought up on which the interest of the day concentrated itself. It arose out of a motion of Mr. Dewar, of Sandwich, to vest the Patronage of the Rectories, which is by Act of Parliament given to the Church Society, in the Bishop of the Diocese. This was met by an amendment to the effect that it should be vested in the present Bishop during his lifetime. A brief but very animated debate ensued, which terminated in the withdrawal of the amendment, and the adoption of the original resolution, the announcement of which by the Bishop was received with a loud demonstration of satisfaction. One or two minor matters were then disposed of, the usual complimentary resolution to the Bishop was passed, and the meeting was dismissed at the hour of midnight, with his Lordship's benediction.

Thus terminated the proceedings of a meeting which was distinguished by a delightful unanimity, no less than by deep earnestness of feeling—a meeting which it is earnestly and confidently anticipated, will be followed by many others, if not so important in their results, yet equally conducive to the welfare of our Jerusalem, and equally serving to illustrate the Divine sentiment, "Behold how good and joyful a thing it is, brethren, to dwell together in unity."

Faithfully yours,   H. H,

Diocese of Huron, C.W., September, 1858.

(*From the Church Journal, November* 10, 1858.)

Extract from Nova Scotia correspondence, containing account of meeting of Diocesan assembly :—

You are probably aware that, according to the Constitution of the Assembly, no measure can pass without the concurrent sanction of Bishop, Clergy, and Laity.

Considerable umbrage had been taken by some opponents of Synods, at the liberty thus given to the Bishop to dissent from the action of the other two bodies, but on this occasion we had a practical example of the exercise of this privilege by the *Laity*, whose dissent *vetoed* a measure concurred in by the rest of the Assembly. This first exercise of the obnoxious " veto " by the Laity, instead of by the dreaded *Episcopos*, caused some amusement. Several important regulations as to the trial of delinquent clergymen, were passed, after due deliberation. Hitherto almost absolute power, in this and in many other respects, had been vested in the Bishop alone, under the Royal Patent, and it is to my mind one of the commendatory features of the Synodical scheme, that thereby the Bishop calls in his clergy and laity to share with him in powers and privileges from which they were before excluded.

(*From the Quebec Mercury, December* 11, 1858.)

MEETING OF MEMBERS OF THE CHURCH OF ENGLAND.

At a public meeting, convened in St. Paul's Church, Kingsey, in the Diocese of Quebec, on the second day of December inst., to express publicly their disapproval of certain controversial and disorderly proceedings, for some time past carried on by professed members of said Church, within the city of Quebec, the following resolutions were passed.

Whereas a certain party in the City of Quebec, professedly members of the Church of England, have of late factiously set themselves in opposition to Ecclesiastical authority, sometimes openly in public meetings, but more frequently covertly and over fictitious names through the public press, and published pamphlets, have much disturbed the peace of the church ; and by misrepresentation, through misguided zeal or visionary apprehension, have done much to bring her administration and clergy into contempt ; weaken the confidence of her members; and distract her unity ; to the great disparagement of our religion, the honor of Christ, and the prosperity of His

Church in this Diocese; holding her up irreverently and contemptuously to the public gaze and ridicule of all who scoff at religion, or have no good will towards our Zion.—It is hereby—

1st. Resolved,—That this meeting convened in St. Paul's Church, Kingsey, in the Diocese of Quebec, and speaking the sentiments of the Anglican Church in this part of the Diocese, review with much concern and regret, the spirit and conduct of the said party, as being at variance with the fundamental principles of Apostolic Christianity; and deprecate their proceedings, as inconsistent with their profession, grievous to all well-instructed churchmen, and meriting the condemnation of all good and unprejudiced Christians.

2nd. Resolved,—That, whereas the said party have put themselves forward as the index of Anglican Protestantism in this Diocese; and have organized a Society and constituted a self-styled " Lay Committee of the Diocese of Quebec ;" we need no such champions of our liberty, we accept not their patronage, we disregard their sympathy : We venerate our aged and excellent bishop, and have full confidence in our clergy ; and we beseech our brethren of Quebec to lay aside their Alexandrian spirit, and return to quietness, peace and good order.

3rd. Resolved,—That, whereas the said party have assailed in a most unbecoming, uncharitable and unchristian manner, the University of Bishop's College, an Institution closely allied with the prosperity of the church in Eastern Canada, and one meriting well of the public, yet struggling against the prejudice of some, the apathy of others, and the difficulties, which in common with all, beset the incipient stages of similar institutions ; and regardless of self-respect, have descended to the use of lampoons, satire, and of vulgar and opprobious epithets against its learned and able professors and the graduates thereof,—We cannot express our condemnation of such unworthy and suicidal conduct without heart-felt sorrow, and sympathy with those who have much reason to expect better at their hands.

4th. Resolved, That although the said party have spared no pains or expense to disseminate their principles far and wide, we have hitherto contemplated their movement in silent pity, regarding it only, as in truth it is, a local faction, or one of those occurrences spoken of in Scripture as temporarily permitted of God, as a trial of our faith and steadfastness.

WILLIAM CARSON,
Senior Church Warden, Chairman.

F

(*From the Quebec Mercury, Decr. 23.*)

ADDRESS TO THE LORD BISHOP OF QUEBEC.

We have much pleasure in publishing the following address to the Bishop of Quebec, from the Mission of Frampton and its dependencies. This expression of feeling, so creditable to that Mission, shows unmistakeably the place which our venerated Bishop holds in the affections of his people. We hope, ere long, to see this example followed by many other country Missions. We may state that this address originated with and was carried through entirely by the laity, and was signed some time before the resolutions of the Churchmen of Kingsey were published in our paper.

To the Rt. Reverend the Lord Bishop of Quebec.

We the undersigned, heads of families, inhabitants of East and West Frampton, Standon, and Cranbourne, respectfully approach your Lordship to offer our expressions of deep sympathy in this time of trial, and to assure you of our unabated confidence in the uprightness of your Lordship's intentions and acts, in the high position in which it has pleased God to place you in the church.

From the public prints, and more recently from your Lordship's " Letter addressed to the Clergy and Laity of the Diocese," we have learned, and with much regret, the opposition which has been offered, by a party in the city of Quebec, to your Lordship's just and liberal views in regard to Synodical action, and the gross misrepresentation to which your conduct has been subjected. For our part, we beg to assure your Lordship of our unshaken reliance on the watchful care and zeal, which for so many years you have shewn in the administration of this Diocese. The fact, that for more than twenty years you have supplied us with a resident Clergyman, though our means were altogether inadequate to his support, shews the kindly interest which your Lordship has always taken in our welfare.

Though poor, my Lord, we trust that we are not ungrateful, and if the support and affection of an humble portion of your Lordship's flock can tend in the slightest degree to lessen the anxiety incident to your high and responsible office, we beg respectfully to assure you of both.

In conclusion, we heartily pray that your Lordship may long be spared to preside over the Church in this Diocese, and that your efforts to promote harmony among all parties in the

Church may be so blessed with success, that we may be all joined together in unity of spirit and in the bond of peace.

(Signed,)   John Dillon,   Andrew Ross, J.P.,
                  Thomas Hodgson,   William Bagley,
                  Edward Anderson, Michael Armstrong,
                  James McClintick,   Churchwardens,

And one hundred and four others, heads of families.

REPLY.

Quebec, Decr. 17, 1858.

My Christian Friends,—I have received with feelings of much gratification, the kind address in which you convey to me the assurance of your confidence in my administration of this Diocese, and your appreciation of those labors in which it has pleased God to use an unworthy instrument for effecting some good in this portion of His Church.

Whatever troubles have been caused by the Episcopal movement for procuring Synodical action, it is a comfort to enjoy the well assured feeling that they are not chargeable upon the author of that movement, either in originating, or in conducting the movement itself, and that they could not have been anticipated as a consequence of any other exercise of the episcopal authority within the Diocese.

It is nothing new, however, in the history of the Church, that men should encounter opposition and misconstruction when they are seeking, in all good will and simplicity of heart, to work for the public good. We can only commit our cause in prayer and faith, to Him who can make all things work together for good, and who can turn the hearts of men, as well as guide the course of events according to His good pleasure. We may well hope that the cause of peace and order in the Church, and the preservation of those principles among us, which essentially belong to the Anglican Communion, however rudely they may be assailed, or however perseveringly undermined, will one day be seen to triumph, as well as that many persons who have been carried away by colorable appearances will correct their own mistakes for themselves. Meantime, I desire cordially to acknowledge the contribution of your own efforts towards so happy an issue.

I am, my Christian friends,

Your affectionate servant in Christ,

G. J. QUEBEC.

Messrs. Dillon, Ross, Hodgson, Bagley, Anderson, Armstrong, McClintock, and other signers of the address.

44

(*From the London Guardian, Feb. 10, 1858.*)

CHURCH SYNODS IN THE COLONIES.

There are three distinct modes of Church government in vogue, and in practice. There is the Episcopal, there is the Presbyterian, there is the Congregational. Each of these has its own advantages. The Church of England is in *theory* what Cicero calls a *temperamentum* of all three. As our State is in theory a combination of the monarchical, the aristocratic, and the democratic, though in practice the latter element has absorbed the first, and part of the second ; so in theory the Church of England has its two Houses of Convocation to represent the Episcopal and the Presbyterian forms of government, and the Parliament made its own Congregational voice to be heard. But since the Parliament lost its specialty as a Church body, it can hardly be said that there is really any Congregational government in the Church. The Houses of Convocation for all practical purposes are still a cipher ; and the whole active government of the Church is Episcopal ; *active*, we say, for no doubt there is an immense amount of inert and passive resistance in the other two elements that makes itself felt for conservation, if not for progress.

Now, all Churchmen have felt the present state of things to be defective—at home, Low Churchmen try to remedy it in their own way by establishing societies on a purely Congregational system, fusing together Bishops, clergy, and laity, and so eliminating the Episcopal and Presbyterian elements from their rank as co-ordinates. High Churchmen, too, at home are divided on the question how they may best remedy the existing evil, Some think that the regeneration of the present form of Convocation will do all that is needed. Others wish to see the laity admitted as a distinct order into the Church's Synods. Such is the state of feeling and of practice here. But abroad in the colonies, all alike, High or Low Churchmen, seem to have come to the conclusion that there is no other way of working the Church system effectually but through the three co-ordinate elements—the Episcopal, the Presbyterian, and the Congregational. The Bishop of Toronto, the Bishops of Melbourne, Adelaide, and New Zealand, have all independently arrived at the conclusion that there is no other solution of the question than by the *temperamentum* of all three on an equal footing. Church Synodical action then, in this sense, is no High Church conceit ; by none but the most ignorant of history can it be called a Mediævalism ; it is no attempt to regain ecclesiastical power, but a simple expression of a principle contained in the theory and idea of the Church of England, and the outward visible body of its life.

These remarks are suggested by the papers relating to the New Zealand Church Constitution that have lately reached us ; from which it would seem that the Bishop has been labouring for ten years past to establish the result at which the Church has just arrived. It would appear that for fifteen years he had been, *malgre lui*, an autocrat, and that no one felt more painfully than himself the evils of such a system, in which all the onus of power and of obloquy fell upon his shoulders alone. There was hardly a clergyman, or a church, or a schoolhouse, or a churchyard in the colony, for the maintenance of which he was not made responsible. If a window was broken in the church, the Bishop was held to blame till it was mended. Gentlemen sat in church with their umbrellas over their heads, because the Bishop, who had advanced most of the money for the building, did not also see to the securing of the saddleboard that had been warped by the sun. To such minutiæ were Episcopal autocrats reduced, and deservedly so, if it had been of their own choosing ; but the position was forced upon them ; and the great duty and labour was to impress the clergy and the laity with a due sense of their own responsibility in regard to the maintenance of their own church in the colony. This was no easy task. The plan proposed was unlike the existing state of things in England ; and there is a strong Conservative feeling in the breast of the most Democratic colonist. It was not then till many other minds, lay and clerical, were duly impressed with the real need of the Church, and after ten years' patient discussion and ventilation of the subject, that at last in May, 1857, two Bishops, eight clergy, and seven laymen, met in Synod for a whole month, and produced a Church Constitution, of which we can only say at present that it seems promising and feasible. Of the eight clergy, four were missionary Archdeacons, summoned to represent the natives, the other four were elected ; the seven laymen were elected deputies from all parts of the diocese.

The main principles of the Constitution are—first, that those three orders are, for all legislative purposes, equal, and nothing can pass into a law without the assent of a majority of each ; secondly, that as long as the Prayer book and the Authorised Version of the Bible remain unaltered by the Church at home, the colonial branch binds itself to the full acceptance of the formularies of the Mother Church and its Authorised Version, but leaves itself at liberty to accept or decline any future alteration made by the Church at home.

This General Synod will depute its powers to diocesan Synods (*) and local vestries, still holding and exercising a supervision over all, and a power of revoking abused authority. As far as can be judged from the unanimity that prevailed throughout the first session, we augur good results for its working. In countries where the Voluntary system prevails, nothing short of the co-operation of all orders will seem to meet its difficulties and dangers. We have the more confidence of this result when we see that the plan devised is in such full accordance with the principles of the Primitive Church, and with the theory, at least, of our own English branch of the Church Universal.

(From the Sherbrooke Times, January 6, 1859.)

One of the great doctrines of Christianity is " Peace on Earth, good will towards men," and happy would it be if the practice of Christians were at all in accordance with the doctrine. But unfortunately this divine precept, so often enunciated, would seem to bear a different interpretation from the literal one, if we may judge by the discord which but too often prevails in every branch of the Church.

How is it that amongst christians so much strife and opposition, so much bickering, so much envy, hatred and malice should be apparent to every eye. It is not merely that sect is so frequently arrayed against sect, but the evil displays itself still more forcibly amongst the followers of the same creed. Surely strife is not a necessary ingredient of the Christian character, for " Peace on earth, good will towards men" was heralded forth as the result of the coming of the Saviour. No ! the evil is in ourselves. If every christian were in his own person to endeavor to heal wounds and reconcile difficulties, rather than by obstinate adhesion to his own views, to create trouble, and widen the gulf between himself and others, whose main objects are after all identical with his own, but who

(*) " The constitution of *Diocesan* Synods to be *similar* to that of the general Synod : but the question of an appeal to the general Synod from the veto of *any one order* to rest with each Diocese to decide for itself." 5th Resolution.

happen to think differently as to the means of obtaining the end, the result would be such as would rejoice the heart of every good man, and the influence of Christianity itself would be far wider and deeper spread amongst the masses of the people.

How can a man or community, with any show of propriety, inculcate doctrines of sobriety and temperance, when the example and the precept are so widely separated?

We are led to these remarks by the perusal of a pamphlet recently issued by the Lay Association of the members of the Church of England in the Diocese of Quebec.

We would ask firstly, is such an association necessary or even desirable? Why in a Christian community put class against class? Are not the interests of the Clergy and Laity identical? Why endeavor to raise up antagonism between the people and their ministers in religion?

But to the pamphlet itself. Grave charges are made against the Bishop, (*) it being asserted that after a certain meeting held in Quebec in June last, for the purpose of determining as to the acceptance or not, of Synodical action in this Diocese, and after the vote of acceptance was passed, further proceedings were stayed by violent conduct on the part of both Clergy and Laity; that a vote of adjournment was carried, in the hope that time and reflection might tend to allay the bitter feelings drawn out, but that in the meantime the Bishop took advantage of the sitting of Parliament to cause an amendment of the act to be passed, authorising and requiring the appointment of Lay delegates to meet in synod, and legislate on the internal

---

(*) *Note by Compiler.*—Notwithstanding this, which seems to be sufficiently plain, the advocates of the Lay Association, in order to disarm opposition, are heard to say, while they are circulating this very pamphlet, that they have nothing to bring against the *present Bishop*, but simply desire to put matters on such a footing as that if he should have an *unworthy successor*, he might be restrained from doing mischief. Surely such inconsistency must be easily seen through. The same parties put themselves forward as the champions of the rights of the laity throughout the Diocese; but no one can read the foregoing extracts, without perceiving, clearly enough, that the object OF THE BISHOP has, all along, been *to secure to the Laity of the country their just rights, of which those who oppose him would have deprived them* by keeping the control of every thing in the hands of a mass meeting at Quebec. Defeated in this attempt, they now endeavor "by good words and fair speeches, to deceive the hearts of the simple," (†) when they profess to be the friends of the people. It is impossible to avoid this conclusion, except on the charitable supposition (which one willingly indulges) that they are deceived themselves.

(†) *Romans, XVI.* 17. *Read the whole passage.*

affairs of the Church.—This is the charge, and a Lay Association is formed, denouncing the conduct of the Bishop and his immediate followers ; letter follows letter in the public press, and a pamphlet is issued, warning the laity that their rights are being invaded and that they must come forward in defence of their religious freedom.

Surely this must be considered as 'somewhat violent conduct, and to the outside observer, would tend to shew the wisdom of not allowing Quebec, en masse, to legislate for the whole Diocese.

To us, resident at a distance from the scene of trouble, the conduct of the Bishop in securing the rights of the Church in the Diocese in general, by allowing representation in fair proportion by delegates from every parish, seems the most liberal policy.

Mass meetings are not the place for calm discussion, and the vital questions at issue can only be met by quiet temperate conduct on 'he part of all.

We are clearly of opinion that the Bishop has in this instance, shown a promptitude and energy of character in applying an immediate remedy to the evil felt, and acknowledged by all, which ought to earn for him the thanks of the diocese at large.

No doubt he f lt that time and discussion, instead of allaying the spirit of discord, was only exciting it, and he would naturally think that another exhibition, similar to that of the June meeting, would do incalculable harm to the cause of the Church over which he presided.

Again, in the appointment of delegates he has only carried out the wishes of both parties. The extremest reformer could not call for more, for the choice of delegates is left entirely in the hands of the Laity themselves.

We have felt it our duty thus to allude to this pamphlet, and we earnestly hope that the good sense of the people in the townships, to whom we more particularly address ourselves, will lead them to avoid joining any exclusive party in the Church ; and when the time for action arrives, let another Christian maxim overrule all their actions, " Whatsoever ye do, do all to the glory of God."